Garrick Cross is devastated when his house is ransacked in an online scam. Somebody posted his address on Craigslist and saying Free for all. They take everything, even his garden hose. He finds his rare, beloved Vendetta guitar on an online auction and bids on it, distraught when he loses the bid by a buck. The police are trying to help him locate his stolen property, but the auction is a done deal. His precious Vendetta is gone. He emails the man who beat him to it, asking if he would consider selling the guitar to him, at a higher price. Micah Drake, a reclusive collector who won the auction says no and is quite rude . . . until they start emailing each other and discover they share the same unusual passions for obscure music and movies. They accidentally meet — or do they? — and Micah overcomes his shyness, telling Garrick he will give him the guitar if he spends a weekend in bed with him. How badly does he want the Vendetta? Garrick agrees, only in spite of their scorching lovemaking sessions, he finds some vendettas are so one-sided. He's falling for Micah and learns that Micah wants him, too. Then Garrick discovers who was behind the theft and starts to falter. Can he let go and trust love again?

The Vendetta
Copyright © 2020 A.J. Llewellyn
ISBN: 978-1-4874-2971-3
Cover art by Martine Jardin

Published by eXtasy Books Inc or
Devine Destinies, an imprint of eXtasy Books Inc

Look for us online at:
www.eXtasybooks.com or www.devinedestinies.com

THE VENDETTA

BY

A.J. LLEWELLYN

DEDICATION

To the great slack key guitar legends, Keola Beamer, The Brothers Cazimero, and Gabby Pahinui, whose music always inspires me.

And to the memory of Rell Sunn, the First Lady of Surfing. Sleep with the dolphins and surf with the angels, Rell. The world is a lot less sunny without you. Xxx

CHAPTER ONE

"You know, Garrick, I think you're being a little paranoid."

I stared at Dr. Vicky Royce and wanted to choke her. From the start, I'd felt she wasn't a good fit for me, and now I was convinced. She had said this more than once. Trust me to find the least sympathetic, least warm and fuzzy therapist in the entire state of California.

She toyed with the long chain around her neck as she inched her legs a little to the side. She often flirted with me, but then counter-punched with a rebuke. At least it seemed that way to me. I hated the way she liked us to sit — very close, facing one another, knees touching. My pal, Sarah Swan, had warned me that Vicky used this intimate method of therapy. Now it just seemed . . . intrusive.

It took me a few moments to calm down. I felt the weight of her stare. She'd already upset me by telling me she'd written a song, inspired by me: 'Moth to the Flame.' The nerve of her! She'd even played it for me in the middle of my session! Was it appropriate for a therapist to use her patients as song-writing fodder and then make them cringe through the end result? I would ask Sarah if this had ever happened to her during one of their sessions.

My therapy had turned into a music critique.

I shifted in my seat.

"Vicky," I said, "I don't think I'm being paranoid. On a scale of one to ten, this breakup with Brad is an eleven."

She rolled her eyes. "I think, once again, you're exaggerating."

I stared at her. Was she kidding? What did she think a bad breakup was? I didn't ask her, because I knew she would highlight her response by using one of her own breakups as an example. A lengthy and *boring* example. Or—God help me—force me to listen to the musical version of it.

The rose incense she insisted on burning in her tiny office started to get to me. She may have been the therapist to writers and musicians all over the universe, but for me, she was a catastrophe. I'd been devastated by Brad leaving me for one of our closest friends, Joshua, and then doing everything he could to turn all our other friends against me.

Brad didn't like Sarah because in his words, she was "a nut." He had tried to turn her, but she and I were working together on a big project for a chain of restaurants. I'd brought her into the deal. She needed me. Brad had gotten to a few people I worked with, but Sarah and I had a bond. I stood, just as Vicky picked up her iPod to flick through and play me another song.

"I have to get going," I said. "I'll listen next week."

She reached for her massive appointment book. "Same time next week?"

"I'll have to let you know." I already knew I wasn't coming back, but I preferred not to have a confrontation in person. I just wouldn't call her again. *Ever.*

Scanning her cramped, warped bookshelves, I blamed myself. I should have known she was the wrong therapist for me, judging by her collection of commercial, paperback crap. She had the worst taste in fiction of any person I knew—even my grandma. And I knew my fiction, being an online antiquarian bookseller.

My mom, up in Santa Barbara, had been unhappy when I called her with my therapy updates. She called Vicky *hard core* and felt she was cruel in her handling of me. My mom knew how badly I'd taken the breakup. Eight years was a long time with one guy, especially a gay guy in Los Angeles. Don't ask me why, but this city was rough on relationships where seventy-seven percent of all marriages ended in divorce.

It had only been three weeks since Brad had left, but with his nasty phone calls and the horrible emails from Joshua, telling me what an asshole *I* was, I felt I had a right to be in the midst of the breakdown I was struggling with.

"Have a great day." Vicky picked up her guitar and barred my exit. "Are you recording this week?"

I hesitated. The guitar was practically in my face. She was desperate to get into the studio, *any* studio, and cadge some recording time. She'd recorded her latest piece of rubbish at her current boyfriend's home studio. Now they were on some rocky terrain. She'd already mentioned a couple of times that she felt *creatively robbed*. I was fighting for my life, trying to think up good reasons to stay alive. She hadn't given me many during our session. In fact, she might just have pushed me over the edge. I was, by nature, a strong man, but like I said, I was under duress.

But she, the great therapist, was being *creatively robbed.*

"Not sure yet," I said, desperate to get out of her office.

She followed me into the hallway.

"I'd love to see you work," she said. It was another of her standard refrains. "I am dying to see the Vendetta."

The Vendetta. It had been the one spark in my few sessions with her. She'd heard from Sarah that I owned one of the original Dean From Hell guitars. Only one hundred and fifty had ever been made. Vicky owned a damned fine second edition Dean From Hell, but it wasn't an original.

"I'll let you know." I stifled the urge to scream and slap her — and her guitar. I paid her the seventy-five dollars I owed for our session. Even that hurt. I was stuck with paying full rent and all the bills on the Toluca Lake cottage I'd shared with Brad until a few weeks ago.

Outside, sunshine hit me, and I felt my body respond. Los Angeles in June could be gloomy, but this day was gorgeous.

Around seventy degrees, the temperature was soft and warm, a slight chill starting on the afternoon breeze. The nasty heat the San Fernando Valley was famous for wouldn't unleash itself until right around Independence Day.

I retrieved my car from the parking lot behind the Century Eight movie complex. I shook my head. The next time I came here would be to see a film, not endure another pointless session with Vicky Royce.

Traffic was heavy and the talk radio show I normally enjoyed in the afternoon had a different, bombastic host, who was irritating. Right wing rhetoric wasn't my thing. I switched it off and pressed the button for my CD player to kick in. I loved the Hawaiian band, The Sunday Manoa, and found myself soothed by the wondrous guitar and double-bass duo of Roland and Robert Cazimero, The Brothers Cazimero. I shot down Laurel Canyon and turned left on Moorpark, heading east. I idled at the corner of Lankershim outside St. Charles church when I saw a dog amble past Angelino's Pizzeria on the southeast corner. I did a double take as the dog glanced inside the restaurant as if he could smell good eats. He ignored the swoosh of traffic and stepped off the curb. I screamed when I realized it was my own dog, Cassady, running along the street.

I almost ran the red light trying to get to him. Not only was this about the busiest intersection in the city, but Cassady shouldn't have been anywhere near the street. He crossed the road, looking disoriented, as cars and buses slammed on brakes.

I knew something bad was going on for my baby to be on the street. The light was about to change, but I didn't care. I threw the car into park, jumped out, and ran for my dog. Cassady ran from me, thinking it was a game. My elderly golden retriever had the personality of a puppy still, but his bad back leg prevented a full run. I grabbed him by the collar and hauled him to my car.

The people behind me honked. I'd had no choice but to rescue my guy. I got him into the front seat and held up a hand in apology. I was the only driver to make it through the green light, and I cringed at the cacophony of horn blasts as I made it to the other side of the intersection.

Cassady sat in his usual passenger seat beside me. He panted heavily, soon tiring of the familiar view. I caught his sad gaze. He thought he was out for an adventure. Going home was so disappointing. He plopped down, his head leaning across the gears to rest on my lap. I would have stroked his lovely, soft head, but I was too busy stressing. My grip on the wheel was ferocious. How the hell had he gotten out of the house?

My second indication of a major disaster was the plethora of vehicles lined up outside my house when I arrived. I finally knew the meaning of the words, *my blood ran cold.*

People were coming out of my house, like a line of sugar ants, carrying my belongings! One guy had a truck fully loaded.

Holy shit!

"What the hell is going on?" I asked another guy, struggling with my unwieldy garden hose.

"Dude, you're too late. It's all gone."

"What do you mean it's all gone?"

"The house." He jerked a thumb over his shoulder and jostled the hose for a more comfortable grip. "The ad only went up on Craigslist a couple of hours ago. These guys are professional movers. They came with special foam packaging for the dishes and everything." His head tilted toward the van in my driveway now backing out. "I bet they're gonna have this stuff on eBay within the hour."

I couldn't move. "What do you mean, it was on Craigslist?"

"Just what I said. Under miscellaneous. A note saying the house was unlocked and all contents were free and everybody should help themselves. The only thing I could get was the hose. And I don't even need one."

"That's *my* hose!" I sputtered. I could hear my dog panting in the passenger seat of my car.

The guy looked at me. "Sorry, dude. Finders keepers."

We wrestled over the hose a moment and I almost cried when I saw another guy coming out with my light fixtures. My distraction gave the hose thief some leverage.

Holy crud on a bagel!

The two men ran down the street, and the line of cars vanished. I ran back to my car and pulled into my driveway to stop anyone else from parking in it. I let Cassady out of the car, helping him to the ground. I hooked my finger into his collar, and we walked inside. It was like a car accident — a moment of horror when it all washed over me. I'd been robbed. No . . . not robbed. I'd been completely stripped of every last thing I owned . . . and many things I didn't. They'd even taken the kitchen sink, my dog's bowls, the fridge . . . even, for God's sake, knobs to the kitchen cabinets.

Cassady circled the usual spot where he knew he could find water and lifted huge, mushy brown eyes to my face. The expression there unglued me. It was as if he asked, *Why Papa? Why?*

His nails on the hardwood floors echoed in the empty house.

I had no good answer for him. I fought off a wave of unmanly tears as my hands shook, trying to get my cell phone from my pocket. I stared at the hole that used to be my kitchen sink. Cassady growled at the same moment I heard a noise coming from my bedroom.

Holy crap, somebody was still in the house!

Tears swarmed my eyes as I pressed the numbers for 911. I swatted at them as Cassady made a run for the bedroom. I heard a shout and ran to the room.

A guy was in there trying to force the screens from my

window.

"911. What is your emergency?"

Cassady had one of the guy's ankles in his jaw. The guy screamed again.

"I'd like to report a robbery. I just came home and found a bunch of people robbing my house," I shouted into the phone.

The guy tried to bat Cassady away, but I pushed his hand away from my dog.

"Don't," I said, pushing him against the wall beside the window.

The full impact of my echoing voice, my totally empty bedroom, hit me. They'd even taken the fucking blinds! Where the hell were all my things? My computers? My guitars?

And oh, no. Where the hell was my Vendetta?

CHAPTER TWO

The man at the window threw up his hands.

Cassady let go of him at my coaxing.

"Hey, don't look at me, man. I came because of the ad."

"I'm sick of hearing about this phony ad," I shouted, ready to beat the crap out of this guy. "I just went to see my therapist and came home to find my dog running loose, and every last damned thing except my window screen gone!"

"If it's any consolation, I can't get the screen loose."

I really lost it then as the 911 operator kept telling me to keep calm. I punched the intruder right in the face. He slumped to the wall.

"This is a citizen's arrest," I said, staring out the window to see my neighbor, Mrs. Satō, peering across her little white picket fence at me.

"Are you okay, Garrick?" she yelled out.

"No, I'm not okay," I shrieked back. "Didn't you see all my shit being stolen?"

"Yes. I called the police half an hour ago."

She gave me this news as the 911 operator asked me if I knew a Mrs. Satō.

"Yes, she's my neighbor. Can you please come now? This is a robbery in progress. I need help!"

Footsteps clattered in the hallway.

I ran out there, Cassady at my heels.

Two uniformed cops walked through my house, shaking their heads in disbelief. One of them led the only intruder I'd caught away from my home and returned some minutes later.

"You didn't place an ad on Craigslist telling people to help themselves to your household contents?" he asked.

"No," I said. "I did not."

"We're going to have to get a detective over here. People are still arriving."

"Yeah," I said, "But it's all gone."

The cops were very nice. They could see I was in shock. I was very touched when one of them got a paper cup out of his squad car and filled it with bottled water for Cassady. My sweet boy bent his head and lapped at the liquid. I started to cry.

"It's okay, guy," one of the cops said, putting a reassuring hand on my shoulder.

But it wasn't okay. They asked me who hated me enough to do something like this. I could only think of Brad and Joshua, but the questions still circled.

Why? Why? Why?

Mrs. Satō came over. The cops thought she was another freeloader and tried to shoo her away. I was grateful they stayed since the thieves kept multiplying.

"Do you have Brad's number?" one of the cops asked.

I gave it to them. And Joshua's.

"Joshua would never do something like this," Mrs. Satō insisted. If you'd asked her a month ago, she would also have said her loving son was a model college student, straight in every sense of the word, and a credit to his Japanese parents.

The police reached Brad. I didn't hear the whole conversation, only snatches of, "If you are responsible, this is the worst robbery I've ever seen. They left the poor guy with nothing. And the vultures are still coming."

Detectives arrived and went around the house asking the same questions. One of them brought in a laptop, showing me the listing on Craigslist.

"You didn't write this?" he asked me.

He was a youngish guy who looked too thin for his suit. Well, that was my immediate impression. He was a mix of Asian and white, and his expression was unreadable.

"No," I said for the umpteenth time. "I did not."

I remembered I had LoJack on my laptop but didn't know the serial number. The laptop, of course, was gone, but I had a flash drive I kept on my key ring. I thanked God I'd done a quick backup of my computer before racing to my appointment.

"Can I have the flash drive, please?" the cop asked. He plugged it into his laptop and up popped my music files and every other damned thing I had on my computer. He located the LoJack information and called the company, organizing an immediate search.

His cell phone rang in seconds.

"This listing was done from your laptop," the cop told me.

My mind reeled. "Impossible."

"At two o'clock this afternoon. One of our IT guys just said so."

I shook my head. "I wasn't here. I had a therapy appointment." I glanced at Mrs. Satō, who looked stricken. This would get back to her nasty little son and my equally horrible ex-lover for sure. "You can check with my therapist."

"I will," the cop said, his large brown eyes connecting with my own.

"Her name is Vicky Royce. I'd write her number down for you, but all my pens have been stolen."

I couldn't keep the venom from my voice. I could hear the uniformed cops arguing with somebody at the front door. Goddamn thieves. They were still trying to rob me!

Craigslist refused to take down the listing until the cop, whose name I learned was Inoue from the terse conversation he had with somebody in their marketing department, told them he would charge Craigslist as accessories to theft. He also said he would personally see to it that the site received its worst publicity ever.

"The listing has been canceled," Inoue said to me a few seconds later. "But it might be up for another thirty minutes."

"Thirty minutes..." I rubbed my hand over my recently reduced mop of hair. I'd cut off all my long, blond hair in a drunken stupor one night. I didn't miss the hair as much as I wished like I didn't look as though I'd tangled with a lawnmower.

"Don't worry, Mr. Cross—"

"Please, call me Garrick."

"We're going to stay right here with you until the tide of home invaders slows down and—oh... she just picked up." Inoue spoke into the cell phone.

"Ms. Royce, my name is Detective Inoue. Thank you for taking my call. You can confirm that your client was with you?" He cradled the phone against his ear and tapped something into his laptop. He listened for another minute. Inoue... *in-noo-ay*... I liked the sound of his last name. My mind drifted. I was a musician so I couldn't help but think in melodious terms. Inoue cut my therapist's rant off mid-flow. He ended the call, his gaze swiveling to my neighbor.

"Mrs. Satō, has your son been here today?"

The poor lady gripped the hem of the white apron she always wore. She paled under his scrutiny, her little toes bunching up between the white plastic daisies on her black zoris.

"He . . . ." She glanced at me, her hand smoothing down the apron frill in her fingers. "He came to see me. He never came here."

Inoue looked at her. "Lying won't help you. This is a major crime. I am charging your son with grand larceny. Do you really want to be charged as an accessory?"

She bit her lip and started talking, again. "He said he needed the house key because he left his schoolbooks here, and Garrick wouldn't give them to him. I . . ." Her eyes pooled. "I'm so sorry, Garrick."

I couldn't respond.

"Did he give you the keys back?" Inoue asked her.

She nodded. "He said he couldn't find the books."

"There weren't any books." I fumed. I glanced at Inoue. "I have an even bigger problem that I need to discuss with you." I glanced at Mrs. Satō. "Alone."

"Where's private?" he asked.

"Backyard?"

"Lead the way."

Outside, I thought I would have a heart attack. My little back yard had been my pride and joy. The thieving bastards had even stolen some of my plants.

"What's up?" Inoue asked. His cell phone rang again. He took the call. After a brief exchange of words, he glanced at me.

"Your laptop has been traced to a pawn shop in Van Nuys. It just showed up on an eBay auction, listed along with some other stuff."

We went back inside, and I felt my horror mounting as my worldly possessions appeared in pristine shots. My clothes, my studio gear, my mom's Tiffany lamps I'd been looking after for her . . . And my beautiful, stolen Vendetta.

"That didn't take long," Inoue said. "eBay's a little harder to deal with. I don't think I can get all these auctions down before they end." He made a couple of calls, and I paced the kitchen. Mrs. Satō looked miserable.

"I'm sorry," she said again.

Inoue came back to me. "You wanted a word?"

I nodded. Cassady followed us back outside.

"My problem is bigger than just my stuff being gone," I began. "I do verification work for a memorabilia company. Right now, I've been hired by the House of Rock restaurants to authenticate some big purchases. I had three boxes containing forty-one items. They've paid a fortune for these things. I don't normally take items off site, but I had an appointment scheduled for seven o'clock tonight with Cynthia Rodriguez, who is an Academy Award-winning costume designer for big movies."

I paused. "As far as I could tell, the items in question were fakes. One T-shirt in particular is alleged to have belonged to John Lennon, but from what I learned yesterday, the type of stitching used on it has only been in existence for fifteen years."

"Oh . . . man, you're telling me all this stuff is gone too?"

I nodded. "Yep."

"Son of a bitch." Inoue ran a hand through his hair. He had a cute cut. Long on top, short on the sides. I felt certain he hadn't given himself a cock-eyed trim. He was exotic-looking and sexy in a square kind of way.

"In my experience," he said, "when gay men break up, it can be worse than a man and a woman."

Fuck. He was a homophobe. All the good things I'd been feeling about him evaporated.

"Assholes are assholes," I said, "no matter what their sexual persuasion."

He opened his mouth, but his words were soon drowned out by the high-pitched hysteria of my prissy landlord.

"Excuse me. I am the owner of this house!" I heard Patrick Prince's voice booming and caught Inoue's glance.

"My landlord," I muttered. God, this was all I needed.

Patrick stumbled outside in his tight, tight jeans and his tiny pink T-shirt with the words *Free Joe Exotic* emblazoned in rhinestones and stopped. "What the hell's going on, Gary? What the fuck happened to my house?"

"Mr . . ."

Inoue glanced at me and I supplied the name. I left them to talk as I returned to the house, my dog at my heels.

I went through each room. The only things left in the kitchen were two tacky plastic champagne glasses at the top of the kitchen cupboard. Oh, so the thieves had some taste.

There were some old cleaning rags, sponges, and detergent under what used to be the kitchen sink.

There hadn't been much food in the fridge, but the appliance had come with the house and was almost new. They'd ransacked the food cupboards. I had some pasta and a bean soup mix left. They'd even stolen my half jar of peanut butter.

Cassady flopped to the floor and whined. I rinsed out one of the plastic champagne glasses and filled it with the remaining bottled water the cops left on the counter. I put it on the floor, but Cassady kept his eyes closed, sighing again, his chin resting on his paws.

"You're right, babe." I stroked his soft head. "Don't look and it won't hurt so much." I sat on the floor beside him, stroking his flank. He rolled away from me, his eyes staring ahead. It's a sad day when your dog gets so damned depressed.

Patrick came into the house with Inoue, who was on his cell phone. I gaped when I realized my prissy landlord was crying. He went out to his car and came back, snapping photos of everything. As I stood, he glared at me.

"The damage is around thirty thousand dollars, Garrick. Under the terms of your lease, you're responsible. I hope you have renter's insurance."

"I did," I said. I took a deep breath. "Brad canceled it. They gave him a refund check, even though I was the one paying for it." I glanced at Inoue. "That's when the horrible emails and calls from Joshua started. These guys . . . I have no idea why, but they've been terrorizing me. I'm the one who got dumped, but they've been harassing me."

"Huh?" said Inoue. "I spoke to them by phone a few minutes ago. They tell me it's the other way around."

I shook my head. "They can tell you whatever they like, but whose house just got ransacked? I've got emails and cell phone calls to prove how ridiculous this whole thing has

14

become."

Inoue studied me for a moment. "I'm not saying I don't believe you. I'm just wondering why."

"Good question," I said. "Maybe you should ask *them*."

"Don't worry, I will."

His cell phone rang. He studied the screen as one of the uniformed cops came into the kitchen.

"News crews heard about the robbery. They're out front."

"Good," Inoue said, putting his cell phone on his belt. He glanced at me. "Thank God for slow news days. I'm going to ask that everyone who stole your stuff should bring it back, no questions asked. I know you have nothing left on the premises, but as soon as you can, you need to put signs on the front door and the back, letting people know the ad was a prank and they need to leave immediately or the police will be called."

It took me a second to digest this news. Just as I'd started reassembling my life, it had all been smashed to shit. I needed to contact my employers and my mom. I needed a different life. Why the hell had this bullshit happened to me?

My thoughts raced.

"I need food for Cassady. I'm afraid to leave the house, though. God knows what they'll take next."

It was a shock to realize I'd said this aloud.

"Garrick," Patrick suddenly said, showing a rare flash of humanity, "I'll get some cardboard from Staples. I'll make the signs. What do you need for Cassady? Just give me a list."

Inoue and Patrick went out front to deal with the news crew, and I stood at the hole that used to be the kitchen sink. I didn't even have a fucking pencil to make a list. I opened drawers and found a couple of knives. They might come in handy, should my despair deepen.

My cell phone rang. It was Sarah, my best friend and work buddy.

"Dude. What the fuck happened? I just saw your house on TV."

I took a deep breath and told her.

"We need to get online and start bidding on your stuff," she said.

"I hope the cops get it all stopped."

"Don't count on it. Our friendly, neighborhood therapist is already bidding on your Vendetta."

I was shocked. "How do you know that?"

"She told me. You've got a rare guitar there, bucko."

"Yeah, I know."

"She has Dean From Hell guitars bookmarked on eBay. She said she knew it was yours from your photos."

I scrolled through my cell phone and found the listing online again. I was even more devastated. *Scarce! Original Dean Zelinsky, Dean from Hell Vendetta Guitar. Limited Edition! Only one hundred and fifty ever made!*

Thank God my mother still kept my important papers at her home in Santa Barbara. I could prove ownership of it.

I sent the seller a message through eBay that the listed item was stolen property. I alerted eBay too. I had no idea how long it would take them to remove the auction, but that guitar was my pride and joy. I found other things that belonged to me—a Les Paul guitar, some studio equipment. Each minute that went by revealed more of my stuff being uploaded. My vinyl collection went up as one unit.

These thieves didn't waste time. I made a list and emailed it to Inoue.

Sarah turned up, looking like a hillbilly angel. I'd never met anyone more beautiful, nor more determined to make herself look like a farm girl. Tall and willowy, she had long, dark hair she kept below her shoulder blades, and she always wore jeans and plaid shirts. Every type of plaid imaginable, Sarah owned. She also wore cowboy boots.

Her thing in life, however, was clothing. She went from one

movie to the next, working as a dresser for some of Hollywood's hottest young actresses. She dressed down so the female stars wouldn't see her as a threat, also so the crew would see her as a drinking buddy.

Sarah carried a horse satchel as her purse, and it always contained red lipstick, a Phillips head screwdriver, and her cell phone. She opened the satchel and removed a spare leash, some food bowls, and a throw rug for Cassady. Like me, she was an animal lover, and our pets came first.

"I like your new Kabuki look," she said, waving a hand around the house. "Shit, not even a chair to sit on?" When I shook my head, she said, "I'll go buy you some. You poor little waif, you."

She drove off as Patrick finished changing my locks. He didn't trust Mrs. Satō next door not to let Joshua back in. Frankly, neither did I.

Sarah returned with two lawn chairs she'd picked up at the drug store and a sack of food from our favorite Thai restaurant, the Rustic Spoon. She'd even bought us each a Singha beer.

"Did you realize they even stole your toilet paper?" she asked, after a trip to the loo.

"No, but they left these very disgusting plastic champagne glasses."

"I'm surprised they left the dishwasher," she added.

"There is no dishwasher. That's a façade."

She laughed. "Boy, is that ever the story of your life, Garrick."

I would have gotten mad at her if she hadn't been so right. We sat in our chairs and ate. Even the wonderful green papaya salad, fragrant, rich green jungle curry, and crab rolls couldn't dispel my gloom.

My cell phone rang. Cynthia Rodriguez, the costume

designer who was supposed to come and evaluate the memorabilia for House of Rock, said she couldn't get near my house.

"There are news crews and the police. Did somebody get shot?"

I apologized. I'd forgotten all about her. I told her what happened.

"Bummer," she said and ended the call.

Between Sarah and Patrick, I got a few home comforts before the evening ended. Patrick brought me a roll of toilet paper and a hideous, Pepto-Bismol pink table lamp. However, this particular beggar could definitely not afford to be choosy.

The cops stayed around until the trickle of scavengers evaporated. Inoue gave me his card and said he'd be in touch. I was left with a donated airbed from the neighbors on my other side and an old blanket I found on the floor of my linen closet.

I closed my eyes as I lay on the airbed on the living room floor, trying not to think about the cost of replacing everything I'd lost.

Unable to sleep, I put a call in to my boss, Eric Walker, at the House of Rock. Inoue had already contacted him earlier, but like me, reached only his voice mail.

All night, the long silence left me listening with a hopeful ear for people returning my stuff. Sleep eluded me. Cassady and I sat out front after a while, and I stared around me. The nights in Los Angeles were very cool. More and more, the city became desert-like. Hot during the day, bone-chilling cold at night. I lived in a nice, leafy neighborhood. A lot of showbiz folks lived here too. One block down on Ledge was Bob Hope's sprawling property. His widow, Dolores, had lived there right to the end, putting up with intrusive fans for decades. I'd had less than a day of strangers marching to my front door and had been traumatized. How had she coped with the constant deluge?

I couldn't imagine how she'd dealt with the daily intrusions of tour buses stopping by to ogle her. Not to mention people who knocked on her door, expecting her to smile for an endless parade of selfies. I wondered if she'd ever felt free to walk around her house naked.

Now that my window treatments were all gone, I sure wouldn't.

Old Mrs. Hope was gone, but the five-acre estate she'd left had been the stuff of legend. It sold for fifteen million dollars last year after being the subject of a lot of legal wrangling and many price drops from its original asking price of twenty-seven million.

I lived close enough that I'd gotten a good look at the extensive grounds with a golf course, putting green, two swimming pools, and a massive guest house.

What a wouldn't give to be over there at this very moment. I had a strong feeling the guest house probably had an intact kitchen sink, and plenty of toilet paper.

I leaned against my wood-veneer front door, hoping that it wouldn't collapse with the way it was making creaky noises. Ten years ago, I'd relocated to New York to be a playwright. Two years later, I drove back across the country in a busted-out lime green Pinto, my brand-new puppy Cassady at my side. I came with two hundred dollars and my dog. I still had the dog, I told people, when I'd spent the last of the two hundred smackers.

Yeah. I still had the dog.

Cassady and I stared up at the stars in the sky. Contrary to popular belief, you could see stars in LA's night sky. Being able to see them in the smog-ridden valley was a good sign. Tomorrow would be a nice, sunny day. I'd named my boy for Jack Kerouac's best friend, Neal Cassady. I'd spent so much time carving a life for myself, paying bills, staying one step ahead of the creditors that I'd forgotten to write. Now, come to think of it, I didn't take too much time to look for stars anymore.

I rifled through my cell phone for the stored number I had for the Griffith Park Observatory's Sky Report. I called it and got a fascinating account of what was going on astronomy-wise.

"At dawn, the brilliant cream-colored planet Jupiter and the golden-hued planet Saturn will gleam in the south as an eye-catching pair . . ."

I sighed. Astronomy was such a romantic science. If and when I got my laptop back, I would start writing again. I would look at the stars and allow myself to dream. I didn't care that Kerouac famously wrote an entire book on toilet paper. I only had one roll to my name. I needed to preserve it. Besides, I was a child of the computer generation. At thirty-four, I was addicted to keyboards.

Sadly, though I'd hoped for a miracle, by midnight the only scavenger who returned was the guy with the hose.

CHAPTER THREE

M y boss, Eric, called me around seven a.m. He was upset about the break-in and the loss of the items I'd been assigned to evaluate.

"Well, we're insured," he said. "Can you come into the office, today? I need to discuss this matter with you."

"Sure thing. Can I bring my dog? I'm afraid to leave him here, in case the scavengers come back and take him, too."

Eric agreed. I rolled over, a deep depression washing over me that I didn't have music to wake up to—my favorite radio station putting a smile on my face—or my sweet, comfy bed to snuggle into for a few extra minutes. The sleep, which had eluded me all night finally overtook me. I closed my eyes, but seconds later, my doorbell rang.

I stumbled to my feet, Cassady taking over the airbed. Through the living room windows, I saw a huge truck parked out front and two guys circling the front of my property.

They caught me looking at them through the window.

"We drove all the way from Chino! We came to get some stuff, but the sign on the door says we can't," one of them yelled. He tried peering into the windowpane.

"No, you can't," I screamed. "Now fuck off, before I call the police."

He gave me the finger. I was still feeling insecure and nervous. I didn't flip him off in return. I was afraid of getting a brick through the window.

I watched them retreat. I made sure they drove away and went back to the airbed. I jostled my dog for space and had just managed to squeeze myself beside him when the front doorbell rang again. I raced to the door, flung it open in a total rage.

"What did I—?"

I stopped. It was Brad.

"Jesus . . . babe," he said. "I'm so sorry."

Up until three weeks ago, he could still make my heart flip like a flapjack on a sizzling pan. His dark eyes and hair still held their allure, but I knew his dark heart now. I shook off the bad thoughts. I wouldn't let him in the house. I *couldn't*.

He pushed past me. He kept muttering, "*Oh my God*," as he saw the damage. I was frightened having him here. I hadn't seen him in person since he walked out of my life, taking what was his—and a lot that wasn't—and his new lover was a headcase.

"You have to leave," I said, afraid to close the door and be left alone with him. I was also afraid to keep it open in case more relic chasers turned up.

"Garrick . . . I'm so sorry," he said again. "They took your family photos?" he asked, fingering the naked mantelpiece.

"Brad, they took everything."

"It wasn't supposed to go this far. I thought . . ." He paled suddenly. "They took the lights?"

"What part of *everything* don't you get?"

"Don't be bitter, Garrick. It's just . . . things."

Things? They were *my* things. "Listen, Brad, I don't even have clean underwear to put on today or a fucking tooth-brush. Your psycho boyfriend set me up. So don't tell me not to be bitter!"

He walked into the kitchen as if he still lived here and spot-ted the leftover takeout cartons on the counter.

"Leaving stuff around with our ant problem, Garrick?" He peered inside and saw there was still some curry left in one of the containers. "Why don't you put it in the fridge?"

I just stared at him, as the realization must have hit him.

"Right. No fridge. Oh. What about the garbage bin?"

"Nope. They took that too."

"This is so creepy."

Having you here is creepier. "Not as creepy as coming home to find people stealing my shit, Brad."

I really wanted him out of my house. Cassady was acting weird. He normally would run to Brad, and I had a bad feeling as my dog trembled against my legs. I felt in that moment that Brad had been a party to this, that he'd been here. Had he been the one to let my dog out of the house? I couldn't speak, afraid, mad, and protective of Cassady all at once. There was nothing left that Brad could take except my dog — or my life. I felt more threatened than ever.

"The kitchen sink." He gestured to it. "Shit. This went too far."

"Yeah. Tell me about it."

He flicked a glance at me. "Does Patrick know?"

"Yes. And he estimates the loss and damage at thirty thousand dollars."

Brad ran a hand over his face as I showed him the paper Patrick left me.

"They stole all the tropical plants he put in the backyard along with the Hibachi." I pointed out the window. "It looks like a bionic mole hit the neighborhood."

Brad didn't say anything.

"Patrick's holding me responsible. Unfortunately, you canceled the insurance policy we had on the house, so he's taking me to court."

He blanched. I wondered if this had been their scheme all along, and I also wondered why he hated me so much.

"Why did you do this to me?" I finally asked.

Brad moved toward me.

"Look, it was a prank, a silly prank. You know Joshua. He's a sweet boy. He doesn't have a mean bone in his body."

"Several mean bones, actually. Cassady was on Lankershim Boulevard. He ran across the road."

"Oh man . . ." He threw up his hands. "I'm sorry, babe. Joshua is just so jealous."

"Jealous?"

He nodded, his fingers moving to my jeans.

"Oh, baby, he's not you."

I was surprised when he knelt in front of me, pressing a kiss right on my package. In the old days, it was a pleasure — his secret love touch. Now it was weird. He lifted his face, trying to fumble at my button-down fly. I slapped his hand away.

"Are you crazy?"

"Jesus, Garrick. I still love you."

"What?" I took out my cell phone and walked away from him. "You have twenty seconds to leave or else I'm calling the cops."

He crawled over to me, trying to rub some life into my cock inside my jeans. I pushed him away and dialed 911.

"Don't do that," he said, getting to his feet.

"I told you. I want you out of here."

He smacked the phone out of my hands, but I caught it before it fell. The call didn't go through. "Get out," I screamed, just as Joshua's mother arrived at the front door.

"Garrick," she called out. She kept pressing the bell. I raced to let her in, Cassady at my heels.

"Are you okay?" she asked, but she was looking at Brad, not me.

"He won't leave," I said. "Maybe you can convince him."

She frowned at Brad. "Didn't you ask him?"

"I . . . tried."

My head swiveled to him. Man, he was gonna give me a blow job in exchange for some favor?

"Ask me what?"

"Joshua's gonna get arrested if you don't drop the charges against him," Brad said. "Please, Garrick. I know this is bad, but I love him."

"Sorry," I said. "It's out of my hands. Your little prank backfired."

A police car rolled up, another car right behind it. I saw Inoue getting out of the second car. The scowl on his face was intense.

"Who's he?" Brad asked me.

"He won't leave," I shouted at Inoue. "Can you get him out of my house?"

Brad screamed. "No! I'm not in the house!"

But he was.

Inoue and the uniformed officer he was with led Brad and Mrs. Satō away.

"Everything okay?" Inoue asked me over his shoulder.

"No," I said. "It's not."

Inoue kept walking, his expression unreadable. I watched him talking to Brad out front. Mrs. Satō scurried away, gripping the hem of her apron as usual, looking petrified of the cop. She stumbled over her own zoris.

I watched the animated way Brad responded to Inoue.

"Calm down," I heard Inoue say. His voice rose. "Garrick's landlord is the one pressing charges. I told you last night that you and your boyfriend are to leave Mr. Cross alone."

I needed to file a restraining order. I saw that now. My mom had suggested it. *Mom.* I hadn't called her last night because I didn't want to worry her. Until the robbery, the campaign against me from Brad and Joshua had been by email and phone calls only. Well, I'd change my number and use a different email account.

Inoue stood over Brad, watching him drive away in his cherry midnight blue 1978 Impala. Inoue held up a hand to me and came back to the house.

I studied him a moment. He had a thing to his walk. Quite a sexy hitch to it. *Stop it, Garrick.*

"The Craigslist ad is completely down," he said as he reached my front door. "By the way, I had complaints from the neighbors that a few of them had stuff stolen during the worst part of the free-for-all and a couple of incidents during the night, so I'm leaving a uniform patrol here for an hour or so. Just in case. This has been the weirdest robbery I ever saw."

"Wow . . . I had no idea they took stuff from the neighbors. Now I feel really bad."

"Did anyone return anything to you?"

"One guy. He'd stolen my garden hose. Well, the landlord's garden hose." I couldn't help smiling. "I guess I could use it on anyone else who turns up. I already had two guys this morning."

He nodded. "Yeah. We got a call." He hesitated. "Did you get some rest?"

"Not really. I kept hoping the bastard who stole my bed would bring it back."

He chuckled. "Sorry. I shouldn't laugh, but I'm pleased to see they didn't take your sense of humor."

"Yeah, what do you know?"

"We got some of your stuff taken away from an eBay listing. We were lucky. It was a professional seller and she was willing to cooperate, but I can't return it to you yet. It's evidence right now. I'll email you a list of what we removed from her office. You were a big help."

"Is my toothbrush one of the things you found?"

He stared at me. "They really cleaned you out."

"Yeah. They even stole the toilet paper."

He suppressed a grin. "I am gonna try to return some essential items, but some of your things have already changed hands. Your Vendetta guitar is up for auction. It ends today. I just checked before I came over. It's already at fifty-thousand dollars and there's six hours left before the final bid."

I wanted to cry. *My Vendetta.*

"My therapist is bidding on it. Nice, eh?"

"I'll have a word with her." His cell phone rang. "We'll try and get those auctions closed as soon as possible. The fraud division is on the case. Like I just told your ex, this is a big case now. Anytime the Internet is used in the commission of a robbery, it's like the mail system. It's a very big deal."

I nodded.

"Garrick, try and have a nice day, okay?"

He stuck out his hand and I shook it.

"Thanks."

"You have my number. You get any more trouble, you call me."

Was it my imagination or did his hand linger on mine? Man, I was so hard up for comfort, I was reading stuff into the smallest, kindly gesture.

Inoue drove off. I leashed Cassady, wondering if it was safe to take him for a walk. I did have a uniform patrol out front. Oops. No, I didn't. The guy was driving up and down the street now. I supposed I could call it a community patrol. I was desperate for coffee and hungered suddenly for toast. I was afraid to take my car out of the driveway, in case I came back to find 'Starving Students' removal service hauling my remaining household items.

Sarah pulled up out front.

"Breakfast," she said, hopping out of her ancient white Ford pickup truck, holding up a paper carryout bag from McDonald's and two giant cups of coffee on a cardboard tray. She also had a card table in the bed of her truck.

If she'd been a guy, I would have asked her to marry me.

Sarah and I sat at the table, wolfing down pancakes and sausages. Cassady ate his dog food, giving me a sullen look from across the kitchen floor.

"I spent a bit of time last night going over the eBay

auctions," Sarah said. "They're almost all still live. There's a couple that ended without bids. When are the cops taking the others down?"

"Don't know," I said, setting aside my bacon for Cassady. "Inoue said some of the items had been removed. But he did say my Dean From Hell is still up there."

"Yep. It's at sixty-five grand right now. Auction closes at one."

"It was fifty K a minute ago." Suddenly, I felt ill. I couldn't even afford to buy the guitar I owned. Shit. Right when I'm meeting with Eric."

She flicked a gaze at me. "How did he take the news?"

"Not well. He wants me to come in."

She shifted in her seat as she sugared up her coffee. Sarah was the type who liked a little coffee with her mountain of sugar.

"I've been meaning to tell you."

"What?" I asked.

She took a deep breath. "You and I both know that almost the entire lot they gave us to authenticate turned out to be fake."

"We *think* it's fake."

She eyed me in her sharp way. "I got an email from Woody Allen this morning. The Foster Grant glasses were not his."

Sarah powered up her laptop. We had kept careful logs of everything and reported each finding to Eric as we went along. My laptop was gone . . . temporarily or otherwise, and even though I had everything on the flash drive, I had no way to access it, but Sarah was my right hand. She had everything. She showed me the email.

We both sat with this information for a minute.

"This is a problem," I said. "You know how he reacted to the news about the T-shirt and every other damned thing."

"Yes." She held up a finger. "So, technically speaking, he

28

lost a bunch of worthless stuff." She clicked onto eBay. "I'm bidding on a bunch of your things. Your guitar is my main focus. Even if it gets so high we can't afford it, I'm hoping the cops will cancel the listing before we're forced to pay a dime."

I would have taken a shower but had no towels. I couldn't brush my teeth or change clothes. I left Sarah in my house to deal with eBay and any new intruders.

"After all the Tae Bo classes I've been taking, I can kick some ass," she said. She lifted one of her long, coltish legs. "Besides, my steel-tipped boots are dying to imbed themselves in some hose-stealing horse's ass."

She promised to look after Cassady, who had now finished marking his entire turf in the backyard. He came back in to resume his love affair with the airbed and the leftover bacon from my Mickey D's breakfast.

***

Eric's office was in an ugly cement block of an office building in the otherwise enchanting Tujunga Village district, a few blocks from my house. I arrived early and decided to peruse the short strip of loveliness. An artful blend of cafés, gelato bars, and intriguing stores, Tujunga Avenue also boasted Vitello's on the corner of Valley Spring. This was the restaurant where actor Robert Blake dined with his wife on the fateful night where she died in a hail of bullets as they left the restaurant.

I stopped at Hoity-Toity, an eclectic store I knew Sarah loved. She'd been so good to me I had to buy her a gift. We'd had coffee at Aroma Café a few days before, and she had salivated over the contents of Muse House Retreat on the corner.

My hope was that the plaid shawl she'd coveted, with the black and white buttons sporting altered landscape photos was still there.

It was. I was even more thrilled that my credit card went

through. I'd had some late-night worries that Brad and Joshua could somehow empty my bank accounts, but Brad and I had always kept our finances separate.

After getting the shawl wrapped, I had moments to spare. I stopped at the drugstore in the lobby of Eric's office building, bought some personal hygiene essentials, found the men's room on the second floor, and slathered on deodorant. I also brushed my teeth. I still got a shock when I looked at myself in any mirror and saw my shorn locks. I looked disgusting, with patches of hair in odd places that I'd missed and dark crescents under my eyes. My normally cheery expression drooped. However, drooping was all I had today.

Eric's office was its usual calamity. He owned rock-and-roll themed restaurants all over the world and constantly juggled memorabilia, shipping guitars and clothing from one location to the next. A fat Elvis-in-his-gaudy-sequins phase costume Sarah had already authenticated hung on a headless statue in the doorway. It was ready to be shipped to Japan.

The Japanese government had demanded papers of provenance on all items sent to Tokyo, which was where Sarah and I came in.

"Dude," Eric said, spotting me from the corner office.

"Hey." I squeezed past the boxes in his doorway and took a seat. His desktop sported a hat from the Jamiroquai shoot for the music video of the song "Deeper Underground" more than twenty years ago.

It looked like something the Mad Hatter would wear. Or *The Cat in the Hat*. I personally thought it would look smashing with the Elvis costume.

"Sherry," he bawled to his latest secretary, and, if I knew Eric at all, his latest hot bed buddy. "Bring the man a coffee."

She arrived a few minutes later, impressing me by remembering I liked my coffee with just a little milk. She was a lovely, waif-thin thing with big lips, whiter-than-white teeth, and pale blonde hair. She was *so* LA. She shoved some boxes aside and closed the door on us. I could no longer hear Simon and Garfunkel singing about "The Sound of Silence".

Instead, I got the sound of sighing from Eric, who stared at the pages Sarah and I had emailed him a couple of days before. The news hadn't been good.

As I'd focused on the musical instruments, Sarah had focused on clothing and accessories. She was thorough, and I trusted her, but to be sure about the clothes, we'd sought a second opinion. In truth, however, all three of us knew by now that Eric's acquisitions expert had forked out a fortune on phony rubbish.

"How many people know about the John Lennon T-shirt, the sunglasses, and" — he took a dramatic pause — "Marilyn Monroe's alleged last swimsuit?"

"You, me, and Sarah."

"So, you didn't tell Cynthia Rodriguez?"

I shook my head. "I told her I wanted to authenticate some items. She's a '70s expert. She is the one everyone looks to for hippie costumes, bell bottoms, you know ... that type of thing."

"But Sarah is the one who found out about all these things, when three people I pay a hell of a lot more money to had no clue they were worthless."

I hesitated before speaking.

Eric was a wealthy, successful guy. He was a good man who gave money to many worthwhile charities. He had a mania for collecting and had figured out a good way to showcase his treasures. Until he'd hired me and Sarah, since his regular staffers were busy, he had no clue about the extent of his fraudulent items.

Frankly, neither did I. Of the forty-one pieces Sarah and I had kept at my house for further verification, more than half appeared to be counterfeits.

"Eric, I don't know what to tell you. I think the margin of error—or fraud—is high. I think in your line of work, a few things will slip through the cracks, but to be honest, we've been working for nine days now, and it didn't take us long to verify or disprove provenance."

He nodded. "I know. This worries me, let me tell you. I hired you because you're a great musician . . . a great studio guy, and people told me you were quite the historian. As you know, I've coveted your Dean From Hell. Did you know it's on eBay? It's going for a hundred grand."

Eric wagged a finger at me. "I knew it was yours when one of my buyers alerted me. You really looked after that guitar."

Jesus, was he *trying* to make me cry?

"You're one of the few guys who still has the original Kiss sticker on the bottom left spike."

"Yeah." Man, he was seriously depressing me, now. I used to look at the faces of the four Kiss members every day on that sticker. It was if they were my friends.

"And the lightning bolt artwork . . . well, you've kept it pristine. I don't suppose you'd consider selling it to me if you get it back?"

I couldn't think. That was my dream guitar. It was made in 1977, nine years before I was born. There had been two previous owners. I didn't . . . I couldn't imagine not having that guitar in my life.

"Think about it." His tone turned gentle. "I understand you've been through a lot the past twenty-four hours. You've done right by us and bringing Sarah on board was a nice addition to the mix."

He drummed the desk with impatient fingers.

"The thing is . . . the three items you returned that you labeled as definite fakes were among my most expensive purchases and now an outside source has verified your assessment."

Wow. It was good to know we were right.

"I'm going to ask you to do something for me," Eric said.

"Shoot." I found my stomach clenching. After what I'd just been through, it might not have been the best choice of words.

"I want you to forget about it all."

For a moment, I gaped at him.

"The stuff turned up. All of it. The police have it right now."

I snapped my fingers. "So that's the stuff they confiscated."

"Yup. I knew you'd be pleased. They say I should have it back in time for the restaurant opening in Tokyo. That" — he flicked a gaze at a business card — "Detective Inoue found the boxes at some woman's storage facility. She says she got it off a guy who has some of your stuff too . . . but the point is this . . . I want you to forget about further authentication of these items. I want to thank you for your time and for your due diligence." He slid an envelope over to me. "This should cover all your expenses."

I opened the envelope. Wow. Sarah and I hadn't finished the job, and I was kinda being fired, but this check was way more than we'd discussed. It was the nicest sacking I'd ever had. Sarah and I would be splitting the check, and it was damned good.

He slid another envelope toward me. "And this is for the lovely Miss Swan."

I almost fell over. She was gonna piss kittens when she saw this.

"Hey," he said, "You think you could set me up with her?"

I couldn't help looking over my shoulder. His secretary was sitting right outside his glass door.

"She is just recreation, Garrick. A snack. Sarah Swan is . . . how do I put it? She's a multi-course banquet, and I'm dying to put on my big-guy pants and give that feast my best shot."

Eeeww! "I'll see what I can do." I didn't want to piss him off before I cashed the check.

Back home, Sarah went into raptures over the scarf and the check and pretended to gag when I mentioned a date with Eric.

"He'd fuck a snake if it had long legs," she said.

Cassady circled my legs as if he hadn't seen me for weeks. I stroked and hugged him and noticed Sarah giving me one of her penetrating looks.

"What?" I asked.

She looked sheepish. "I have some news for you, too."

"Good or bad?"

"Good. You lost the eBay auction for the Vendetta."

"That's good?"

"That part isn't, *hombre*. The second part rocks. Say, it is *so* weird coming into your house and not hearing music."

"I keep going to press the iPod dock and remembering it's gone. But please, don't digress."

"Oh. Well, the guy who bought it kinda liked the story about your robbery. He wants to meet you. He said maybe you could convince him to let you buy the guitar back for what he paid for it."

I hesitated. "How much?"

"Two hundred and eleven thousand."

I felt tears hovering. Man, it sucked to have to buy back my own guitar — especially when I couldn't afford it. Not in a million years.

"Hey, slick, I know it's shocking. That's why I contacted the buyer. I thought I'd shame him into letting you have the guitar back."

She fingered the soft plaid of the shawl and put it over her shoulders. "I've been emailing him, pretending to be you. He was a real ass at first. Then he got friendlier."

"How did you manage that?"

She flashed me a guilty look. "I sent him your photo."

"My photo? And he wants to meet me?"

"Of course. His name is Micah Drake. He's a bit of a recluse. Lives up on Topanga. He wants to meet you, and he's suggested dinner."

"Dinner?"

She looked shifty-eyed.

I got a sudden bad feeling. "Sarah, what photo did you send him?"

She hesitated.

I was mortified when she scrolled through her iPhone and showed me a photo Brad had sent her of me as a joke. He called it my modeling shot, only I was no model. I was lying in our bed . . . well, my ex-bed. And I was naked, my big, hard cock exposed to the world.

CHAPTER FOUR

"Garrick? Speak to me."

I stared at her, slitty-eyed. "If you weren't the only friend I have left in the world, I'd let you have it."

She shrugged. "He seems cute. Look."

Sarah showed me her laptop screen and yeah, he was. Cute.

"You sent him a nude photo of me!" I spluttered.

"Dude, you are so hot. I'd do you if you played for my team."

"I'd do you if I did, as well." I was confusing myself with the do's and don'ts of our conversation.

I read the email exchange. Micah Drake had suggested meeting for dinner the following night at Inn of the Seventh Ray on Topanga Canyon.

After embarrassing me by sending the nude come-on shot to him, Sarah had coaxed a photo from him. He was standing against an old fence, and he was hot. He had dark hair and eyes, a mysterious, exotic look to his features. His glossy locks appeared to have a close relationship with excellent scissors and hair-care products.

"He's a weirdo," she said. "I checked him out on Facebook. He likes obscure movies and music . . . he's just perfect for you."

"Thank you, I think."

"I gave him your number. He said he'd call."

"You gave him my number?" Was she kidding? This was LA. Bad things could happen to you if you gave people too much personal info. Then I remembered the bad had already happened. Maybe my tide was turning.

My cell phone rang. It was a 310 area code but I didn't

recognize the number. I took the call.

"Garrick?"

"Yes, who's this?"

"Micah." He had a warm, rich voice. "Micah Drake."

My heart skipped a beat. Was he going to take pity on me, let me skip the bullshit meal, and let me have my guitar? My thoughts raced. He'd bought stolen property but may not have known it was. Could I persuade the seller to give him back his money?

"Um . . . the thing is . . . I checked out your story online and you really were robbed yesterday. I kinda feel bad that I'm ah . . . taking advantage of your situation, so here's my suggestion. Let's meet now. Come over for a late lunch or maybe an early dinner. Do you know the Inn of the Seventh Ray?"

"It's my favorite restaurant in the entire universe," I mumbled.

He chuckled. "Another thing we have in common. Can you make it say . . . five-thirty?"

"Yeah, sure."

"Let's have dinner and talk. I'll be the guy sitting at a table for two by the creek trying to hide the boner he's had ever since he saw you naked."

I made it to the restaurant on Old Topanga Road a little after five. Sarah had been keen to hang out with Cassady, but then took him home, which left my house empty. Well, I couldn't babysit it forever, and I couldn't expect Sarah to, either. I knew I was taking my chances, but decided, what could they take? My toiletries? I took the remaining portion of the toilet paper. Just in case.

I was early, but LA traffic was so notoriously difficult to predict. Though it was a forty-minute drive normally from my house, the traffic could slam an extra hour onto the travel time. I was so nervous, I dovetailed into the little bookstore on the premises. The Spiral Staircase had a unique collection of books, music, incense, crystals, and a genuine hippie vibe that was a hangover from the '70s.

"Wow," a voice said. I looked to my right. It was Micah. He was early, too.

He was even more stunning in person. Now I was really nervous. He looked incredibly sexy in pants and T-shirt that showed off all his muscular assets. I looked . . . well, I didn't know how I looked, really. I'd allowed Sarah to shop for me at Macy's, bringing me home jeans, shoes, underpants, and a V-necked cashmere sweater she said looked hot with nothing under it. Not my usual style at all.

"You look hot," he said. "Is that cashmere?" His fingers touched my arm, and I felt a jolt of something. His hands were beautiful. Two things I liked about a man—his voice and his hands. I tried not to think about his hands on my body.

"Are you really enjoying that angel statue?"

"Excuse me?"

He pointed to the statue.

I was rubbing its head. "No." I grinned and started to laugh. "I think I'm nervous."

"I think you are, too. You want to get a drink?"

"Sure." Were my new shoes squeaking?

We walked outside, and actually, I missed the little angel. Rubbing its head had been so comforting. I thought about rubbing the head of Micah's—*stop it, Garrick. Get the guitar. Get some music back in your life.*

The waitress at the edge of the Buddha fountain led us to a table. Micah didn't like it. She let him pick and choose until he settled on one of the stone tables built into the base of a massive walnut tree. It overlooked the creek that circled the restaurant but had some privacy too.

"Thanks, Amelia," he said.

I felt a little more relaxed that he knew people here. So, he really was a local.

"Garrick, I don't have the guitar yet. It's arriving next Monday."

I frowned. "Arriving? From where?"

He shrugged. "The seller bought it off one guy who bought it off another guy."

"So soon?"

"It's a hot guitar and we all negotiated on Jack'd."

"What the hell is Jack'd?" My head was swimming with all of this.

"A hook-up site." He turned bright red. "For gay guys. Anyhow, I think the Vendetta's in San Francisco right now. It's coming via UPS."

I nodded. Inoue had told me some of my things had already changed hands. Man, this had been a fast transaction, though. How had it reached San Francisco so fast?

It was hard not to cave in to depression as I looked at the menu. I'd so hoped to take my guitar home. I was such a Pollyanna.

"How did you come to acquire the Vendetta?" he asked.

I shrugged. I didn't feel like sharing the story with a stranger. It felt too much like singing for my supper, or in this case, my guitar. It was a personal story. I needed a drink. I realized I hadn't eaten anything since breakfast, and I was starving.

"Can I get you a drink?" Amelia asked.

Around us, all the tables were empty. I saw far in the distance on the raised patio, a man and two little girls taking their seats at a table. Daddy's night out with the kids.

"Do you like red wine?" Micah asked me.

"Love it."

"You like cabernet?" On my nod, he smiled. "Will you allow me to make a selection?"

"Sure."

I was stunned when he went for the 2002 Trefethen Napa

39

Valley cabernet. It cost over two hundred dollars a bottle.

"Dinner's on me," Micah said. "I love this vintage. If you like cabernet, this one is like angel's poo. And I already know you like angels."

I laughed, in spite of myself, remembering the way I'd rubbed the angel statue in the store.

We ordered dinner, and I was surprised when we both went straight for the Angel Hair Arrabiata with heirloom cherry tomatoes and wild salmon.

"You really do have a thing for angels, don't you?" Micah swirled the wine in his glass, sniffed it, then sipped. "Very nice," he proclaimed after several seconds.

Amelia filled our glasses two-thirds of the way and we sipped. God, it was so smooth. Like butter. I had to be careful, or I'd wind up drunk for the long drive home.

Micah and I had similar tastes. He ordered the California flatbread, which arrived sizzling and tasty, laden with fresh feta cheese, avocado, olives, and organic oregano. I bit into a slice and groaned with pleasure. It was orgasmic. Man, it had been too long since I'd had sex. After a couple of bites of the wonderful homemade bread, I reflected on how long it had been since I'd *had* sex. Two months.

The last five weeks Brad and I had been together, he'd come up with one excuse after another not to fool around. I picked up my glass, took another sip, bit into my bread, and remembered, with mounting shame, the way Joshua had turned up late one night demanding that Brad tell me the truth, that they'd been lovers for months.

"Penny for your thoughts," Micah said, refilling my glass.

"I'd get more on eBay."

He laughed. "You're funny. I like that in a guy."

The conversation flowed, but I watched his sneaky refills. I didn't trust the guy. Hell, I didn't trust *any* guy. I switched to mineral water, but I still felt giddy until the pasta started to deaden the effects of the stunning, unforgettable wine.

"So tell me how you got the guitar," he said, filling his own glass with the last of the wine. There wasn't a bite of bread or a sliver of onion left on our plates.

"My dad bought it for me," I said. "Just before he died. We went to a guitar convention . . . one of the really early NAM shows in San Diego. I was ten years old."

"What year was that?"

"1996." I fiddled with a nut that had fallen from the walnut tree.

"Go on."

"He was dying. He had cancer. He wanted to get me something I would never forget. I wanted to be a guitarist. It was my passion. He never tried to talk me out of it. My dad was thirty-six and I was losing him. I still miss him every day, Micah. That guitar . . . it was like I still had him with me." I swatted at a fat tear streaking down my cheek.

"I still remember the guy who sold it to us. Oh . . . man, I haven't even told my mom yet. She'll be devastated."

He didn't say anything for a moment. I remembered the vivid blue of my Dean From Hell. It was the sexiest thing I'd ever seen in my whole life. The seller recited the attributes like a catalogue. It had been created for guitarist Dimebag Darrell. The seller pointed out the V-shaped neck, designed for faster playing, the Bill Lawrence L-500XL pickup in the bridge, two traction volume knobs, custom burn marks on the tips of the headstock, a master tone knob, and the gorgeous rosewood fretboard.

I just loved the blue color, the groovy shape—almost like a psychedelic rocket ship. It had two owners, a father, son . . . and then, me—a gift from a dying father to his son.

"Why were they selling?" Micah asked.

The question depressed me. It meant he was interested in its provenance. In keeping it.

His hand reached over the table and stroked mine. He toyed with my fingers in a provocative way, touching the pads of my fingertips with his. Our fingers entwined.

"The seller didn't really want it," I said, feeling a surge of heat that reached my groin. I was sadly in serious erotic distress.

"The mania for 1970s stuff wasn't so huge then," I said. "I think the guy was embarrassed by the guitar. He was more into acoustic stuff. My dad got it for a deal."

Micah's long fingers stroked from my wrist to my fingers. It felt so nice.

"Coffee?" Amelia asked.

"Yes, please," I said.

"Not me," Micah said. "I'm enjoying the buzz."

He talked me into their artisan cheese plate and then assembled the almost erotic array of cheeses for me, handing them to me in bites. There was a rich, creamy brie on thick, sweet honeycomb. He handed me a perfect, plump, sugar-dusted blackberry atop a slice of aged white cheddar. A bite of stilton swiped with quince jam. He was a charmer, that's for sure.

Charmers charm snakes, a voice inside me warned.

"I'm willing to give you the Vendetta," he said, "for a price."

I sure wanted to know the price but was beset by the urge to pee. I excused myself. In the tiny men's room, which contained no doors, only billowing, filmy curtains, I peed like a racehorse. I heard footsteps. In the small mirror to my right, I caught a glimpse of the new arrival. Micah. We exchanged smiles in the mirror, and then he was all over me. His hand moved to my cock and I jumped. I stopped peeing. His fingers ran over the length of my shaft, his mouth moving to my throat.

"You can have your guitar back," he said. "On one

condition."

His tongue slid across my neck.

"What condition?" My voice came out squeaky. Great, Garrick. Really seductive.

"I want to spend the weekend in bed with you."

Did he think I was a hooker? Sleep with him in exchange for my guitar? Surely the cops could get it back for me without my having to resort to prostituting myself. On the other hand, I was afraid a flat-out no would lose me the Vendetta for good. I had to bide my time.

"Yes," I said, as he moved his head and claimed my mouth in an all-consuming, fire-to-my-heart-and-cock kiss.

The kiss would have ended up in some instant, just add water, man-on-man sex had somebody not rustled the curtains as they walked in. Micah and I broke apart, both of us out of breath. It spoiled the mood, that's for sure. We zipped and washed up and returned to the table. He glanced at the check and put some cash on the plate. When we left, he walked me to my car.

"I have an awesome house," he said. "Come and spend the weekend. We'll order great food. We can go out if you like." He leaned into me again and gave me a kiss that sent my brain spinning out into the universe. Wow. He had the kissing thing down. I couldn't remember the last time Brad and I had *really* kissed.

"See you Saturday," he said, rubbing the heel of his hand against my now engorged cock. "I'll email you my address."

I nodded, hooked my finger around the collar of his shirt, and stole another kiss.

"Garrick," he whispered.

"Yes?" I whispered back.

"I really, really, *really* fucking like you."

"Micah, I like you too."

He watched me drive away, raising his hand as I turned

the corner and moved back up the long and winding Topanga Canyon heading north. It was a fun street by day, but treacherous at night because it had no streetlights and turned pitch-black after sunset. You had to concentrate. As a kid growing up here, I'd seen cars plunge over the side into the ravine far below. I knew the road pretty well, but I'd had two glasses of wine, and I'd just been kissed.

God. The man's kisses . . . If he could unravel me with a kiss, he was gonna completely unglue me once we were naked. The more I thought about it, the more I liked the idea. I took out my cell phone to call Sarah and let her know I was on my way home, but, as usual, there was no cell reception in the canyon.

By the time I crested over the canyon onto the valley floor, the cold night air had whipped me into total sobriety and my passionate haze had evaporated. My cell phone reception clicked in, and I checked my messages. I had been heading to Sarah's apartment in Hollywood to pick up Cassady, but her excited voice filled my car as I plugged the cell phone into the radio jack.

"Hey, doll, I'm at Rusty's for the night."

Rusty? Oh man . . . she was seeing him again?

"Cassady's with me, and he's having a blast hanging out with Buster."

Buster was Rusty's basset hound. He was Cassady's buddy. Oh, suddenly I felt a swell of warmth. I'd never liked Rusty, but I adored the guy's dog.

"So, Cassady's my alibi for getting out of here early in the morning." Her voice dropped. "How was dinner?"

"He says he will give me the guitar if I spend the weekend having sex with him."

"Will bone for tunes," she said.

Yeah, whatever. The thought didn't thrill me.

She started to laugh. "Buster and Cassady keep humping

each other. They are so gay. Night, babe!"

I felt a sense of utter desolation. My house was not the same without Cassady inside it. His spirit was so huge. I couldn't face going home to an empty house—a truly empty house—without him, so I passed the Vineland exit on the 101 Freeway and kept going, taking Cahuenga and exiting south.

At the Fat Cat Club, my favorite karaoke bar, I was surprised to find parking out front. I'd stay and listen to a couple of songs and then head home.

Whoever was singing had a great voice. To my amazement, it was Detective Inoue. He had the crowd on its feet as he sang, 'Can I Steal a Little Love.' He was doing an incredible job of it, too. One of the waitresses caught my eye and swung by me, her overflowing tray perched on two fingers.

"What can I get for you, Garrick?"

"Iced tea, please," I said, suddenly parched. Inoue finished his song and came off the stage to raucous applause. He came right over to me. Man, he was a guy of many talents.

"Hey, you," he said, reaching for my hand. We clasped one another, and I felt genuinely pleased to see him.

"What's your first name?" I asked him, "Or should I call you Detective Inoue?"

He grinned as the waitress returned with two iced teas.

"On the house, fellas." She winked at me. "I saw what they did to you, Garrick. Totally uncool."

I tried to slip a couple of bucks into her chock-full tip glass, but Inoue brushed my hand away and put in a couple of fives. She blew him a kiss and took off.

"My name's Makoto, but people call me Mak." He spelled it out for me.

"Mak. I like it."

"Thanks." He sipped his tea. "How are you doing?"

The girl who'd jumped on stage was murdering Donna Summer's 'MacArthur Park.'

"You know, when I first saw you yesterday, I thought I'd seen you in here before, but I didn't recognize you because of the hair."

"Yeah. I shaved it all off."

"I like it." He glanced at the singer, who got more laughter than support.

"Wanna blow this Popsicle stand?" he asked, when she launched into the brutal homicide of another innocent melody.

"Sure." I finished my iced tea in record time.

Outside, I was glad to get away from the noise and the over-warm clubroom. We walked down a couple blocks to Genghis Cohen, a fantastic Chinese restaurant that also showcased hot local talent. It was standing room only. Mak got us a couple of bottles of water, and, in between some decent sets, we talked. On our way back to our cars, I told him about the guitar and about how Micah had bought it for almost a quarter of a million dollars.

I did not tell Mak that Micah wanted my ass in trade.

"That's weird. There's something hinky about that whole set-up."

"There is? Like what?"

He grinned. "I like you, and when all this is over, Garrick, I'm gonna hit on you so fast, your head will spin but right now, I can't discuss this investigation with you."

"Oh."

"I did find your bed. That should put a smile on your face."

Only if you're in it. Man, I must have had some testosterone slipped into my cheese plate. I lusted after Micah and now Mak. His words surprised me. I had no idea until we were in the club together that he was gay.

"You had any problems at the house today?"

"I wasn't around for most of it."

"Well, come on, I'll follow you home and make sure

nobody's there to steal those sexy lawn chairs you've got goin' on in the living room."

I laughed. "Aren't they exquisite?"

"Hey, if nobody else takes them, I get first dibs."

"They're all yours."

He followed me home in his Dodge Neon. I wondered whether it was state-issued and decided to ask when I got the chance. Cahuenga Pass was almost empty as we headed back into the valley. Los Angeles goes to sleep very early. Almost everybody works in the film business and many businesses cater to that crowd. It's hard to find a place open after eleven, which is why places that have musical venues are usually packed.

Outside my house, I idled for a moment, afraid to park in the driveway. Holy crap. Not this again. The lights inside were blazing. I could see somebody moving around.

My cell phone rang, my heart pounding in my chest as I croaked out a hello.

"Garrick, it's Mak. Is somebody supposed to be in your house?"

"No, they're not."

"I'm calling for backup. Don't move."

He had no fears on that score. My dog wasn't home, and Cassady's protection would have been the only thing to induce me to go inside.

A rap on my window made me jump.

CHAPTER FIVE

"Mak, you scared the crap out of me."

"Sorry."

My front door opened and my mom came out in a nightmare ensemble of tight pink leggings and a faded *Paddle Faster, I Hear Banjos* T-shirt.

"Garrick," she screamed, oblivious to the late hour. "Where the hell have you been?"

I stared at her. "Mom!"

As I got out of the car, she slapped my arm.

"Don't 'Mom' me, you little wretch. When were you going to tell me about the robbery? I had to watch it on YouTube!"

"I'm sorry."

"No, you're not."

Mak leaned against my car.

"Mrs. Cross, he's had a rough couple of days."

She swiveled her head to him.

"And who the hell are you?"

I introduced them, and she calmed down a little.

"There's no room for both of us to sleep on that airbed," she said. "Sarah let me in, and then she went on a date." She scowled, her expression spooky in the dim night light.

"She's back with that idiot, Rusty."

I glanced at Mak who stared at my mom, as if mesmerized.

"Yeah. She told me she took Cassady with her." I sighed. "I can sleep on one of the lawn chairs."

"No, you can't," Mak said. "Garrick, you got no rest last night. Look, I don't live far. Come to my place and camp on the sofa."

"Fuck that," Mom said. "I'll come home with you. My bratty son can sleep on that god-awful air bed."

I smothered a smile when I saw the look of dismay on Mak's face.

"Does she snore?" he asked, as she raced inside for her purse and shoes.

"Like a freight train."

"You owe me," he said, slipping his arm around me for one warm, wonderful moment.

"I look forward to settling the debt."

It was hard to walk away from him, but I took a strange comfort in knowing he wouldn't be out scoring with my mother on his sofa. Damn he was sexy. He might not have had Micah's high-octane seduction skills, but he was real. That was it. He was sexy and *real*.

I couldn't believe that in the space of twenty-four hours I'd lost almost everything, but somehow, landed two hot guys.

I didn't know which one I liked more.

Right now, it didn't matter. I needed sleep. I went inside, bolted the door, threw myself on the airbed, and didn't wake up until Sarah was pounding on the window several hours later.

"You sleep like the dead," she grumbled when I opened up the backdoor to her. Cassady cantered in smelling like incense, which he always did when he went to visit Rusty. Back in the days when Rusty and Sarah were *in lurve*, the days when things between them were good, Cassady and I often spent time over at his Mulholland Drive house.

"How was your booty call?"

She uncapped a coffee and sipped it. I lifted the second cup out, added a container of cream, and watched the emotions skid across her face.

"He's using cocaine again."

"Oh, man, I'm sorry."

She looked devastated. "And then, this morning, I was leaving and the biggest rattlesnake I've ever seen was right outside his house—right across the bottom step. I've never seen a snake that big, Gar. It was easily six feet long. It had so many rattles on it. We think he was an old guy. Rusty shot him."

I didn't have any judgment on that issue. Rattlesnakes are a bad thing in California. There had been an epidemic of them on canyon trails and in some of the more rural neighborhoods. With the destruction of so much wild habitat, there were fewer small animals for the rattlers to munch on.

Sarah, however, looked devastated. "He blasted him right in the middle and the thing wouldn't die. It was dead. I mean blasted away, but it kept twitching. He said it would happen for about an hour."

I stood looking at her. As far as I could see, Rusty had done the right thing. He'd done what he had to do to protect Sarah and Cassady.

"Don't you see?" she said.

"No, I guess I don't."

She rubbed her thumb across the rim of her Styrofoam cup.

"It was a metaphor for my relationship with him. He blew me away. Shot me to shit with lead, and I won't let it die. I'm still twitching . . . clinging to it. I don't want to cling to him anymore, Garrick."

I was so proud of her, even as she dealt with a fresh wash of grief. I was relieved Sarah was finally letting him go. I took her coffee away from her, put mine down, and took her into my arms.

"How did you get over Brad?" she asked, when the sobs finally subsided.

I wiped at my own tears. I never could let a friend cry alone.

"It's been hard. What he did to me with the robbery made it a bit easier to let go."

She pushed herself back from me, swiping at her wet

50

cheeks with the back of her hands.

"I feel guilty admitting this, but I've talked to him a couple of times . . . before the robbery."

"Yes, you told me."

"No . . . I mean, I had dinner and lunch with him and Joshua."

I didn't know how to respond to that.

"It was misguided of me. I hoped to convince him to come back to you. I think you and Brad are a great couple."

"We were. We had our time. It's over now."

"Is it that easy for you to let go?"

"Have you had a good look at my house, Sarah? He hasn't given me much to hold on to."

The front doorbell rang. Sarah ran to answer it. I stood, trying to absorb the shock of what she'd told me. I didn't know how I felt about her socializing with Brad and Joshua.

My mom walked in with Mak, who held a box of pastries from Natas, the addictive Portuguese bakery on Ventura Boulevard.

His gaze sought mine, and my heart flip-flopped. I lifted my coffee cup to my lips and missed. Damn. Somebody needed to get me a sippy cup.

Sarah hugged my mom, and the two women talked about how they'd redecorate my house.

I had no desire to redecorate. I wanted to get out. Start again. I needed to move away from the scene of the crime.

Mak leaned over and finger-brushed some coffee away from my chin.

"Bad news, I'm afraid."

I gazed at him. "What sort of bad news?"

"The guy who bought the guitar on eBay wants proof that it's yours and your mom tells me she has no idea where the purchasing papers are. As a matter of fact, she says she thinks she threw out all your papers."

I blinked. *Shit.*

"Say something," Mak said.

"Nothing to say."

"Garrick, is the guitar important?"

"Yeah." I stared at my mother, who was busy talking about manicures and pedicures with the least girly girl I knew.

"My dad gave it to me," I told him.

"I know. I also know what the buyer wants you to do to get it back."

My cheeks flamed. I could feel it. How did he know? He glanced at my mother, and I saw the chain of command. Sarah must have told my mom, who told Mak.

"Are you gonna do it?" he asked.

"I don't know."

He glanced at my mom. "Have lunch with me. Let's talk about it."

I met him at Aeirloom Bakery at one o'clock. It wasn't my favorite place to eat, but it was quiet. Mak seemed down. He'd held back so much about the investigation and he was more reserved than he'd been the night before.

"This sucks," he said more than once, as our conversation ranged over books, movies, our families, his last relationship . . . and then we cycled back to the Vendetta.

"Why do you think your mom threw away your papers?" he asked. "I couldn't believe it when she told me."

I'd been thinking about it all morning, and two things came to me. She was an obsessive hoarder who went through manic bouts of tossing out everything. Somehow or other, she always over-filled the empty spaces again. I explained that to him.

"She kinda said the same thing to me."

"I think she was also jealous of the guitar."

Mak gazed at me, curious. "Really? How so?"

"She feels she didn't have a touchstone after dad died. I had the Vendetta."

"Wow." He looked shocked. "But didn't she get everything else? The house . . . money?"

"Oh, yes."

We paused, biting into our smoked salmon eggs Benedict.

"Were you surprised when I told you she'd destroyed your papers?" he asked, taking a forkful of hash browns.

"Not surprised. I was disappointed."

"Me, too."

I couldn't eat anymore. "My mom never got over losing my dad. I wish you could have known him. He was amazing. I'm not just saying that because he's dead. I mean it."

I took a deep breath.

"Micah Drake asked me about how I came to own the Vendetta, and I told him the story. Not all of it . . . some of it still haunts me."

He stopped eating. I'd never really discussed this with anyone else, except my mom.

"The guy who sold the guitar to my dad . . . well, his dad bought it for him. The guy who sold it really didn't want to sell it, but he was a newlywed, and his wife wanted to travel. She wanted to get rid of all his bachelor stuff. She thought the guitar was ugly and silly, and he said he did, too."

"But you didn't believe him."

I grinned. "You're absolutely right. My dad . . ." My voice shook. "Some days I can talk about him, some days I can't."

"It's okay," he said.

I fought off the demon tide of emotions.

"I want to ask you . . ." He laid his fork on the plate and took up his coffee cup, glancing at me over the rim. "No, I want to *beg* you not to fuck this Micah guy for the Vendetta, but I'll understand if you do."

Mak looked miserable, as miserable as I felt.

"After we bought the guitar and we got outside, my dad made me promise that I would never settle. He told me to hold onto my dreams—for both of us. I feel I let him down because I did settle in my relationship with Brad. Even when I knew, deep in my heart, that it was over, I held on because I didn't want to be alone.

"But I never settled in my career. I followed that dream and it's worked for me. I can't let the Vendetta slip away. I lost Brad, but I love my father more. I feel . . . like I'm losing him again if I just let it go."

"Oh, Garrick. Christ. I am so sorry this happened to you."

My eyes swam now. "Do you think I'm wrong? I mean, I don't know what I will do. Any idea who the seller is?"

He shook his head. "No, I don't. I'm a cop, and I am a man who is deeply . . . in like with you. I knew you were wonderful when you showed sincere feeling for your neighbors getting stuff knocked off when you'd just lost *everything*.

"I've called in every favor I could to get that guitar back for you. I have computer guys working on it. Believe it or not, traces don't happen as fast as they do on television. I have to get permissions and warrants and probable cause and . . ." He put his cup down. He hadn't even taken a sip. "I feel stupid and useless that I can't help you any faster. I want to put a stakeout on Micah's house Monday to grab that guitar."

"That would work."

He shook his head. "I can't get permission. It's not a stolen person. It's a guitar."

Yeah. I shook my head too. I thought I'd go to any lengths to get the Vendetta back, but I didn't want to lose Mak in the process.

I wouldn't ask. I *couldn't* ask if he would still want me if I went through with it. We weren't an item . . . yet, and as I'd already learned, there were no guarantees in life.

Micah called a couple of hours later. He wanted to start early.

"Come today. If it's as good as I think it's going to be then we're just getting a head-start on something wonderful."

I took a deep breath. I could have said no and ended the whole thing right there, but I guess my snake still twitched and wouldn't let go.

"Okay," I said.

My mom felt so bad about throwing out my stuff, she said she'd take Cassady home with her to Santa Barbara.

I thought this was a great idea. I'd drive up there and spend a couple of days with her after the weekend was over. Maybe I could go through some boxes and see if I could find the lost papers.

Mom demanded that I give her Micah's phone number and address.

"This is Los Angeles, honey. I don't want you winding up a sex slave in some deviant's dungeon."

She had no judgments, I was relieved to find. She just felt bad that she had tossed out my papers.

"Call me tonight," she said. "Let me know you're okay."

Once again, I headed west toward the ocean. I got there fast and found his house perched high on a hill overlooking the outdoor amphitheater of the Theatricum Botanicum. I could smell jasmine and pepper trees on the air, a heady combination.

Micah's house was beautiful by Topanga standards. The neighborhood ran the gamut from decrepit, spider-ridden shacks to stunning, state-of-the art homes. This one ran somewhere in between. I saw lush trees bordering the property, a profusion of flowers and plants lining the stone pathway to the door. I took in the horse corrals to the left of the house, and as I turned back, a figure moved away from the huge bay windows. I squeezed past his black Porsche Boxster in the driveway.

He opened the door before I even had a chance to knock.

"Get in here," he said.

I felt my breath catch in my throat, and he was on me, raining fiery kisses all over my face and neck. I couldn't breathe, but I didn't want him to stop. I felt his tongue running along my lips and tongue, and I melted.

He took me inside, his hand cupping my ass. He held me to him. His body was warm and hard, from what I could feel. He dropped to his knees, surprising me with his impatience. He took my cock out, sucking it instantly. I stared down at him. It felt so wonderful to feel another man's mouth on me again. I just gave in to the sensation.

Heat spread through me fast. I tried to ease him back, but he was a cheat. His tongue flicked at my leaking cockhead, pressing into the slit, making the flush of fire roar from my throat to my balls. I came hard, in and around his mouth.

"Bed," he said, leading me by my still erect cock to his bedroom. We stripped our clothes off in record time. I could smell bamboo incense and felt a faint breeze coming from somewhere. I realized it was from above and looked up to see a massive skylight, the window cranked open just a little.

"It's like a treehouse," I marveled, when I saw the proliferation of green from his balcony doors, the windows, and peeping through the skylight.

"That's what I call it," he said, pushing me to the bed. He rolled me onto my belly. The sheets were warm, and I knew they were expensive from their silky feel. He pushed me up to my knees and buried his face in my ass. I knelt, knees apart, wondering when was the last time Brad had taken me with such earnest desire . . . months . . . oh, God. What had happened to Brad and me?

Micah licked and sucked at me, slapping my ass occasionally. I never liked slapping much, but his touch was light, erotic. It only served to inflame my already acute need for his cock in my ass. He slathered something cool and wet onto my hole. Lube. Thank God. I heard the ripping of a condom package, and then he was poking at me. He entered me so quickly, I gasped. Discomfort soon gave way to total pleasure.

I reached between my thighs to stroke my cock, but he urged my hand away.

"No, don't do that. I want you to come just from what I'm doing to you. I want you to come because my cock is making your ass feel really good."

His words hardened my cock, tightening my hole. I thrust against him as he invaded me. He held my hips, giving me a total lower body workout. The only thing I hated about rubbers was that you couldn't feel a guy exploding in your ass. I was about to be proven wrong. His pace quickened, his sweat fell on my ass and back, his hands slid up to my shoulders, rubbing down as his cock swelled deep inside me.

"Come all over the sheets . . . I wanna see how good I make you feel."

I felt him lean back a little, and my cock rubbed against his expensive linens. What he was doing to me, the nasty way he talked to me, fired me up until I saw red spots, swirls of bright lights flooding my brain as I came too. He thundered against me, again and again.

"That was amazing." He kissed the middle of my back.

He stayed in me, and I felt him getting hard again. My cellphone rang, but I was pinned underneath him. I was too far gone to care what earthly matters might be pressing. It kept ringing.

"Somebody wants to get hold of you badly," Micah said, moving into me again. Damn. He was hard, and so was I. His hands moved under me, and he stroked and squeezed my cock and balls. He gently slapped my ass. He knelt behind me, his legs spread. I felt like he was splitting me in two, but I couldn't stop meeting his thrusts. I screamed into the pillow as I came in his hand. He pulled out of me, ripping off the rubber.

"Turn over," he demanded, slipping on a fresh condom.

I rolled over, opening my legs to him. He fucked me again, coming hard, telling me how good my ass felt. He stayed in me until he slipped out, and I shook in his arms. He sucked my cock as if he couldn't get enough of me. He jabbed two fingers into me, even though my ass was starting to hurt, and I came again.

Later, we showered together, and I loved the bamboo and lavender body shampoo he used. I knelt before him, sucking his cock and was disappointed when he pulled away, coming all over my face.

"I love to see come on a man's face," he explained.

Back in bed, we hugged and kissed until it was late. His hands never left my cock and ass, and I let him play with me.

"Are you hungry?" he asked.

"A little." I smiled up at him lazily.

"Then I need to feed you."

He got up, opened a drawer, and held out a fistful of restaurant menus.

I picked out Cholada, the Thai food menu.

"You have good taste. They take forever to deliver, but you're worth it."

We went nuts picking out dishes to share.

"Want to go there and watch the water from a window table?" he asked.

I did not. I'd just had my ass royally fucked and was quite content to stay in bed. He called and ordered the food, but after half an hour, he got impatient.

"I'm gonna go pick up the food. I like the idea of you here, naked and wanting me. You won't leave, will you?" he asked.

"Of course not."

He kissed me a couple of times. He produced a pair of handcuffs, but I balked at those. It was the first moment I felt truly uncomfortable in his presence.

"When I get back, I'm gonna cuff you to the bed posts and fuck you all night long, okay?"

"Sure," I said, but the idea suddenly filled me with dread. Handcuffed? All night long? It had been great breaking the drought, but every instinct in me screamed *get out!*

He threw on some clothes, and I waited until I heard him drive off. I hopped out of bed and hunted for my clothes. I found my jeans, my shoes, but not my T-shirt. I hunted everywhere. It was cold, and I had so few clothes left to call my own, I decided I'd borrow something from his closet.

I ran my fingers through the packed shirts and tops clogging the racks inside it and touched something hard. I couldn't ignore it. I felt guitar strings. I pulled at it, shocked to find it was my own, precious, immaculate, intact Dean From Hell guitar.

CHAPTER SIX

I called Mak.

"Garrick, I've been trying to call you. One of your neighbors taped the whole robbery from the time it started, but didn't bother turning the evidence over to us. He posted it on YouTube."

"Yeah, my mom said she saw it there."

"This guy, Micah . . . he was one of the first people to show up. I recognized his face from the photo Sarah showed me. She's the one who alerted me to the YouTube video."

Now I felt enraged. He'd had the guitar all along!

"Garrick, are you there?"

"Yes." My voice came out a strangled whisper.

"Is it really your guitar?"

"Of course it is. I'd know my own guitar anywhere." I studied it for nicks and scratches. None. One string was loose. I resisted the urge to tighten it.

"I don't want to encourage you to steal it, but it's your guitar to begin with. Garrick . . . my advice is take it and go."

Go? I heard the sound of a car rolling up. *Crud on a bagel.* Micah was back.

"He's here," I said, suddenly fearful. "He lives on top of a bloody mountain. I don't know how to get out of here. He said he wanted to handcuff me to the bed."

"Are you fucking kidding me? Garrick . . . get out of there, now!"

My mind went to pieces when the front door opened.

"Don't do anything stupid, baby, please," Mak said. "Oh, fuck. I hear him calling you. Tell me where you are."

"Too late," I whispered. "Stupid is all I seem to do these days."

I ended the call and stepped into the closet. Micah came into the room as I slid the door closed.

"Garrick?" he kept calling. "Hey, hon, I got the food."

I heard him leaving the room. Some higher force, don't ask me what or who, propelled me to open the closet door and run. I caught a glimpse of Micah in the kitchen. I got to the front door and heard him behind me. I clutched my guitar.

And ran.

I heard him shouting my name and hurtled down Topanga Canyon. I stuck to the side of the street, slipping onto the soft shoulder a few times, and the voice in my head kept screaming, *run, run, run.*

And I did.

I was running downhill away from my car, in the opposite direction I should have been going in, but I glimpsed the Pacific Ocean ahead of me and then I saw it. A police car. It stopped as I ran to the middle of the road, waving my arms like mad.

In spite of my relief, I was dismayed by a crack at my fingertips. My beloved, precious guitar broke at the neck. It had been one of the big problems the Dean From Hell routinely suffered. I'd always prided myself on keeping that neck intact.

"Garrick Cross?"

"Yes," I said, relieved as the cops put me in the back of their car. Mak had called them. Mak was once again on my cell phone.

"I broke the guitar," I said.

"Garrick, it doesn't matter. It's still yours. It's still your touchstone."

"I never allowed myself to play it," I said. "Now I never can."

He talked to me until my cellphone almost lost its signal outside Micah's house. It was shocking to me to learn Micah had many of my possessions. I held onto my broken guitar as Micah called me next. My whole body shook as he screamed at me. "You ruined it! You ruined everything!"

My cellphone battery died. I was terrified he'd come after me. Did he have a gun? I drove away quickly, hoping I wouldn't need my phone during the journey. The canyon was dark and desolate. I rarely came to these parts late at night and every time another car's lights approached from behind, I panicked. Was it Micah? Would he rear-end me? I was grateful when I hit the freeway and had had never been so happy to see bright lights and wall-to-wall traffic.

At home, Mak was waiting for me. I wished Cassady had been there, but it was just me and Mak.

And the Vendetta.

"Do you forgive me?" I asked him repeatedly.

"Do you forgive me for not figuring it out sooner?"

We lay naked except for our underpants, and it was excruciating to be separated by the thin fabrics we wore, but I couldn't have sex with him. I would have felt totally slutty, having just been with Micah.

Mak held me all night and I felt his warmth and his protectiveness. It might have been against LAPD protocol, but in the protocol of right human relations, it was good. It was perfect. He didn't stop holding me all night, his mouth seeking mine whenever I woke up.

In the morning, we looked at the guitar.

"It's a straight, hairline fracture. I bet we can get it fixed," he said.

That same day he arranged to return all my important things—my bed, my computer. His dad knew a guy who got me a new stainless-steel kitchen sink. The house was taking shape. I didn't know if I wanted to live here anymore, but I did know I wanted my landlord to have his house back in the condition in which he'd rented it.

"You're a man of principle," Mak said. "I so admire that." We made a list of things to do over the coming weeks—replanting, buying light fixtures, replacing all the little things I kept discovering were gone.

And then I got a call from Eric, who had seen the news and heard all about the broken guitar.

"I know a guy who repairs Vendettas," he said. "Take it over there. It's a gift from me."

Mak and I drove over there and left the Vendetta in the guy's shop in Sun Valley. He said I could collect it in a couple of days.

"It won't affect the playing at all," he assured me. He wasn't surprised when I told him I'd never played it, that it was my pride and joy.

He looked at me with understanding and with pity.

"When I give this guitar back to you, I want you to play it. They should all be played. Only the guys who truly love these guitars still have them."

"Don't worry, I'll make sure he plays it," Mak told him. For a cop, he had the most amazing, loving, musical heart.

"We should play and sing together," he said to me when we left.

"I can't wait," I responded.

I wanted to go to my mom's in Santa Barbara and pick up Cassady. Mak wanted to come with me. We stopped twice on the way to kiss, pulling over on the edge of the freeway.

I'd made him wait. The man deserved a reward.

A Metro truck pulled up behind us, the driver concerned that we'd broken down and needed help. Mak was embarrassed to be a cop getting caught kissing another man on the 101, but I rewarded him with kisses, and, I thought, a pretty decent blow job, once the Metro guy left us alone.

All night I'd felt Mak's hard cock at my tailbone, but he hadn't touched me. Now, he let me roam around his pants and gasped as I licked his cock, once I got my greedy fingers on it. Cars zoomed past us as I enjoyed the taste of him, the thrill of the speed outside versus the slow movement of my tongue on his lovely, surprisingly thick shaft inside his car. I loved knowing I had kept him so excited all night.

His ass shot in the air when he came in my mouth. I wanted him to come that way for the rest of our lives. Twice more we stopped so I could suck his cock, the third time we climbed into the backseat so we could sixty-nine.

"You make me feel like a teenager," he said, kissing me.

My mom and Cassady greeted us once we arrived.

"What took you so long?" she griped. "That should have taken you two hours at the most. You've been on the road five and a half hours!"

She'd made salad and crab legs for lunch. We sat outside, admiring the ocean view, and Mom told us how tons of people were arrested once they'd been identified and located, thanks to the YouTube video.

According to Mak, Micah had listed a bunch of my items online and admitted he had been playing with me at first— then he saw my photo.

"Yeah, that photo." Mak rolled his eyes.

"He told the police that he was obsessed with you. Now he's gonna get some serious time. He was in cahoots with Brad and Joshua. Did you know Brad's mom had the nerve to call me saying Brad still loves you? Like you need a guy like that in your life."

Mak smiled. "Don't worry, I'll have him shot."

After lunch, we took Cassady for a walk on the beach.

"When we are old men, we'll look back on all this and

laugh," he assured me, hugging me as he tossed a stick for Cassady.

Yes, he was right. Who knew that in losing so much, I would find everything, including the desire to play and man-handle my Vendetta.

"I love life, you know," Mak said as we headed back to my mom's house, the thought of some pre-dinner fumbling high on our mind.

"Life has an interesting way of meting out natural justice. You didn't deserve to get robbed, but out of it came so much good. I got you, and you have your guitar back."

"And I have you," I said. "Without the robbery, I wouldn't have that. And, I wouldn't have my guitar."

He stopped. "How do you figure that?"

"You didn't judge me. You understood. I told you a lot of things about me—about my dad—I never shared, even with Brad. You understood. You didn't like that I went to Micah's, but you never judged me."

"No," he said. "But my plan was to send snipers to his roof if you fell in love with him."

I laughed. For the first time in days, I really laughed. Mak held my hand tighter. I couldn't remember the last time something so simple had made me feel so good.

"Can I interest you in some ice cream?" he asked, as we heard the familiar whine of the ice cream truck's 'Happy Birthday' melody. "I'm thinking we deserve a treat. I like dou-ble-chocolate dipped cones. Can I talk you into it?"

I brought his hand to my face and kissed the knuckles. "Sweetheart," I said, "you can talk me into *anything*."

YOU MAY ALSO ENJOY THE FOLLOWING FROM EXTASY BOOKS INC:

The Haven
A.J. Llewellyn

Excerpt

Being a father isn't easy. Being the gay father to a little boy who simply wanted his mom to bring cupcakes to school for his birthday should have been easy. But my life isn't like that. And apparently, I've passed on this unfortunate gene to my sweet little boy.

On the morning of his third birthday, my son, Julio, awoke at the crack of dawn. And I mean crack. Actually, being fall, I was certain it was still the middle of the night. The sun certainly thought so, as did my lover, Josh.

When Julio stormed in and jumped on us, we fell out of our new sleigh bed.

"What the hell!" Josh hollered. "Earthquake!"

One glimpse of Julio's frightened eyes calmed him down. This jumping on the head thing was new. Julio's see-sawing emotions were not.

He knelt on the bed as we covered ourselves quickly, putting on trousers and tops. We slept in underpants when it was our turn for visits with Julio, but still . . . Being scrutinized by Child Protective Services hadn't been that long ago. We were still nervous.

I checked the time. Nine minutes to five. Really? Didn't my son have an 'off' switch? I looked at him. His chin wobbled dangerously.

"Happy Birthday!" I flung myself at him.

"Happy Birthday!" Josh echoed.

Julio laughed and laughed as Josh, and I hugged, tickled, and kissed him. His new puppy whined from the crate.

She doesn't have an 'off' switch, either.

"Can I let Thor out?" Julio asked.

"No!" we shouted in unison, but it was too late. He slipped out of Josh's arms and quickly released his partner in crime. The twelve-pound barrel of white fur hurtled out of the crate, licked Julio's face clean, then squatted and peed.

All over my nice, new hardwood floors.

She did the big hunch for what I imagined would be a gigantic poop, but I grabbed her just in time and got her out the back door.

Thor gave me a sullen look, sniffing every blade of grass in our pocket-size yard before deciding to finish what she started. I wish she would be so choosy in our house. I actually think the dog's emotional problems have a lot to do with the fact Julio had insisted on calling her 'Thor,' a masculine name.

"She likes it, Daddy," he'd insisted when we found her at the mobile dog adoption on Hollywood Boulevard. A Bichon Frise, she'd been turned into Dogs Without Borders by her owner for the usual crappy reason; she had to move, and her new apartment didn't allow pets.

Almost a year old, Thor wasn't housebroken. She was afraid of everything but turned out to be the sweetest dog I've ever met.

Thor did her thing, and we went back inside.

Julio sat at the breakfast bar, his hair sticking up at odd angles. "Daddy Josh is making pancakes!" He looked so excited. Thor went nuts until I popped her onto the bistro chair beside Julio.

Josh glanced at me. "Daddy Josh will gladly make pancakes, once he finds his utensils. Where the hell do you suppose she put the measuring cups?"

She was Carina. My ex-best friend and mother to my son.

Thanks to her legal machinations, Josh and I got Julio on alternate weeks. We got him Monday, and on Sunday we'd hand him over to Carina. The catch was, she had put pressure on us to accept a little-known California law called Bird's Nest Custody. It means that Julio lives in one house and never has to move. Each week, one parent moves in; the other moves out.

I'd been forced to split the costs on a house for Julio. He was worth every dime. It was dealing with his mother that was difficult. Carina found the three-bedroom, one-and-a-half bathroom house on Craigslist. Josh and I had gone to view it with her, and all three of us had been shocked at how cheap it was. Located on South Sierra Bonita between Olympic and Pico, it's one of the few houses in the area. Everything else is apartment buildings.

We snapped up the place, thanks to the distressed owner's urgency to sell. He'd been in the process of foreclosure and went for a short sale.

Josh and I soon discovered the mid-century home had many problems, including bad plumbing, druggie neighbors who yell and fight all night, a dubious mental health care residential property across the road . . .

And of course, we have to share the space with Carina.

Josh and I had bought a townhouse in West Hollywood, and the weeks we leave Julio with his mom, we head home, to sleep dreamless sleeps. The arrangement was exhausting, but as Sunday mornings creep around, we're anxious to see our boy again.

Carina has a condo on Sunset and Julio was the first to inform us about her new boyfriend. Since he was not an established parent, he wasn't allowed to sleep over at the Bird's Nest house by the family court judge's ruling.

Apparently, Alfredo — the boyfriend — thought rules don't apply to them. Julio said Alfredo sleeps over often.

"He snores, Daddy. But I like it. He sounds like a choo-

choo train!"

I hate the guy, and I barely know him. I hate the Bird's Nest situation. So does Josh. But Julio thinks it's 'super cool, Daddy.'

So does Carina.

She rarely buys groceries, knowing Josh and I do. She frequently breaks things and never mentions it. She just leaves these, and other little surprises for us to find when it's our turn to nest. She moves stuff for the hell of it. She ransacks the pantry and wine cellar. She lets Julio's laundry pile up for us to do.

And she doesn't keep up crate-training the dog, who finds new and ingenious places to do her thing.

I had to find those damned measuring cups.

Josh adores Julio, and I knew he badly wanted to make our kid the best birthday breakfast ever.

Julio looked at me. "Can you find the cups, Daddy?" His bleak expression tore at me.

Josh and I checked the usual drawers and pantry shelves for the elusive items. I glanced out the window and caught sight of the clutch of stainless steel cups sitting beside the barbecue. I raced outside. Evidently, Carina had been barbecuing and just left everything there. Platters, plates, utensils, and glasses were covered in ants. I sighed. She'd also left dishes in the kitchen sink.

I gathered everything, raced into the kitchen, rinsed off the items, except the measuring cups, and stacked it all in the dishwasher.

"Yay! Daddy!" Julio was excited again.

ABOUT THE AUTHOR

A.J. Llewellyn is the author of over 300 M/M romance novels. She was born in Australia, and lives in Los Angeles. An early obsession with Robinson Crusoe led to a lifelong love affair with islands, particularly Hawaii and Easter Island.

Being marooned once on Wedding Cake Island in Australia cured her of a passion for fishing, but led to a plotline for a novel. A.J.'s friends live in fear because even the smallest details of their lives usually wind up in her stories. A.J. has a desire to paint, draw, juggle, work for the FBI, walk a tightrope with an elephant, be a chess champion, a steeplejack, master chef, and a world-class surfer.

She can't do any of these things so she writes about them instead.

A.J. started life as a journalist and boxing columnist, and still enjoys interrogating, er, interviewing people to find out what makes them tick.

How to find/friend me:

email: ajllewellyn@gmail.com
website: www.ajllewellyn.com
www.facebook.com/aj.llewellyn
www.twitter.com/ajllewellyn
Newsletter sign-up: ajllewellynnewsletter@gmail.com—each month I give away a free ebook!